THE SESAME STREET
TREASURY

Featuring Jim Henson's Sesame Street Muppets

VOLUME 10

STARRING
THE NUMBER
10
AND THE LETTERS
P AND Q

Children's Television Workshop/Funk & Wagnalls, Inc.

WRITTEN BY:

Linda Bove with
the National Theatre of the Deaf
Michael Frith
Jerry Juhl
Emily Perl Kingsley
Sharon Lerner
Nina B. Link
Jeffrey Moss
Robert Oksner
Ray Sipherd
Jocelyn G. Stevenson
Norman Stiles
Jon Stone
Daniel Wilcox

ILLUSTRATED BY:

Tom Cooke
Mel Crawford
Larry DiFiori
Mary Grace Eubank
Michael Frith
Harry McNaught
Ruth Marten
Joe Mathieu
Marc Nadel
Michael J. Smollin
Maggie Swanson
Bob Taylor

PHOTOGRAPHS BY:

Neil Selkirk
View-Master International Group

Manufactured in the United States of America   15   14   13   12   11
ISBN: 0-8343-0052-4 (set); 0-8343-0062-1 (vol. 10)

The Monsters' Picnic

Herry, Cookie and Grover
are going UP the hill
to have a picnic.

Herry is playing UP in the tree.
Cookie and Grover are DOWN on the ground.
Herry is OVER Grover...

...and—Oops!—Grover
is UNDER Herry.

The monsters are sitting AROUND
the picnic blanket. They are
ready to have their picnic.

Hortense is IN the picnic basket.
The picnic is IN Hortense.

The picnic blanket is IN Herry.
The picnic basket is IN Cookie.
Grover is going DOWN the hill to buy a hot dog.

PLEASE COME TO MY PARTY

Oscar the Grouch stuck his head out of his trash can to see if anyone had thrown out some good junk. Just then, Grover came walking by with a present in his hand.

"Hello, Oscar," Grover called. "Are you going to the party?"

"What party?" Oscar asked.

"Cookie Monster's birthday party," Grover answered. "It's starting in two minutes."

"Birthday party?" Oscar said. "No one asked me to come to a birthday party."

Oscar felt bad because no one had asked him to come to the party. But he didn't want Grover to see that his feelings were hurt, so he said, "I hate yucchy parties. I'm glad I wasn't invited. Who wants to wear a dumb birthday hat and eat horrible cake and listen to everyone sing stupid 'Happy Birthday'? Now just scram and leave me alone." And he slammed down the lid of his can.

When Grover got to the party, Cookie Monster asked him where Oscar was. Everyone was there but Oscar. Grover told Cookie that no one had asked Oscar to come to the party.

"Oh no!" said Cookie Monster. "This is horrible mistake!" Cookie ran to Oscar's

trash can and knocked on the lid.

"Go away," Oscar screamed, "I'm not home."

Cookie Monster kept banging until Oscar popped his head up. "Oscar," Cookie said, "there's been a mistake. You didn't get my birthday invitation. It must have gotten lost."

"Well, I don't like birthday parties anyway. So forget about it," Oscar said.

"But this is very special birthday party," said Cookie. "It's *my* birthday party. Please come, Oscar."

"No!" yelled Oscar. "Go away!"

Cookie Monster was very sad. He started to walk slowly back to his party.

Oscar saw that Cookie was very sad. "Hey, wait!" he said to Cookie. "Don't get so upset. I'll come to your old party. I don't want you to start crying. I even have a rotten old present to give you."

Oscar did not let Cookie Monster know, but he was very happy now. Cookie had not forgotten him. Cookie Monster and Oscar went off to the party together.

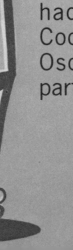

for Cookie

illustration by Ruth Marten

Mind your P's and Q's!

It's bedtime. Prairie Dawn has just gotten into her pajamas and is about to get under her quilt and go to sleep. Can you find all the P's and Q's hidden in her bedroom?

The Count Has a Bad Dream

One night the Count had a bad dream.
In fact, he had a terrible dream.

In his dream, the Count was outside
raking leaves. "Aha," cried the Count.
"Look at all these lovely leaves. They
are falling down very fast. Of course
I will count them all. I will have a
wonderful time, because there are *so
many* wonderful leaves to count.
I can hardly wait. So I will begin.

"One beautiful leaf. Two beautiful
leaves. Uh . . . two beautiful leaves. I
said that already. Ummm. One, two . . .
what *is* this? I can't remember what
comes after two. How can I count
all these beautiful leaves when I can't
even count? There must be some
mistake. I, the Count, not able to
count? Ridiculous! I will count again.

"One lovely little leaf. Two lovely
little leaves. Oh, rats and bats! What
comes next? I cannot count! This is
the worst possible thing that could
happen! The Count has *forgotten how
to count!*

"Shhh. Do not tell anyone. But what
shall I do? I, the one and only Count,
must remember how to count. I will
go to my favorite restaurant, the
Numeral Diner, and order a bowl of
delicious number soup. I will look at
all the lovely little numbers in the
soup—and then eat them. *That* will
help me remember how to count."

The Count put down his rake and
went off to the Numeral Diner.

"Hiya, Count. What'll it be
today?" the man behind the counter
asked. "We've got some French fried
17s on the special."

"Ah, good afternoon. I will have a
large bowl of number soup, please.
And make sure that it has a lot of
numbers, please."

As the Count ate the big bowl of
number soup, he was sure that
seeing and eating all those numbers
would help him remember how to
count.

"Ah, that was wonderful. Now I

feel much better. I will go outside and count all the cars.

"Oh, look at all those cars zipping by. I can hardly wait to count them. Here I go. One speeding car. Two speeding cars. Uh... ummm... two speeding cars. Er... cobwebs and candlesticks! I cannot *remember*! The number soup didn't help me remember. This is terrible! This is horrendous! This is also not nice. The Count *must* count again. I know. I will go to the number store and buy a big bag of numbers. That will help me remember how to count.

"I will have two dozen assorted numbers, please," the Count said to the salesperson in the number store. "And do not bother to wrap them. I will use them here."

The Count took all the numbers and played with them. Then he lined them up and looked at them. Finally he said, "Yes, yes. I am sure that seeing all these numbers has made me remember how to count. I am going

right outside and start counting again.

"Yes, yes. Look at all the people walking by. Perfect! I will count all the people. One nice person. Two nice persons. Ah... umm.... Two nice persons. Oh, no!... I have forgotten again. I cannot count any more! What am I going to do?? I know. I will go to the number factory, where they make all the numbers. That will help me remember how to count."

So, in his bad dream, the Count went to the number factory. He went to the number assembly line, where they were putting together millions of numbers. One woman was fitting crosspieces on number 4s. A man was assembling rows of the number 8.

The Count walked up and down the number assembly line, looking at all the big and little numbers as they were being put together.

"Oh, what a wonderful place this is!" cried the Count. "I love the

number factory. I feel so wonderful that I am sure that now I remember how to count. I am going outside right now and start counting again."

The Count left the number factory and saw all the trucks outside, bringing material to make the numbers.

"Trucks! All kinds of trucks. I will count them immediately. I love to count trucks. One terrific truck. Two terrific trucks. Umm. . . . Two terrific trucks. Oh, darkness and dungeons! How could this happen to me, the Count? I must count again. I know. I will go back to school and learn how to count again. What a clever Count I am!"

The Count went into a school and found a class that was learning how to count. He sat down with all the children and listened to them learning how to count. When they went out to play during recess, he stayed in the classroom. He studied the numbers on the blackboard. When the children came back to the classroom, the teacher called on the Count

and asked him to stand up and count to ten.

"Oh, counting to ten is so simple," the Count said. "And now that I have studied here in your school, I can count to five thousand and ten. But you asked me to count to ten, so I will do it. I will count ten children! Here I go. One . . . two . . ."

The Count stopped. "But . . . but . . . this is impossible. I cannot count past two! I . . . I must be dreaming."

And, of course, he *was* dreaming.

At just that moment, the Count woke up. He sat up in bed, shaking all over.

"Oh, what a terrible dream. I was dreaming that I forgot how to count. But I must go back to sleep again to find out if I ever remembered how to count. What if I never remember how to count?"

The Count put his head back on the pillow, pulled up the covers, and said, "One sheep, two sheep, three sheep, four sheep, five sheep . . ." and fell asleep.

ERNIE PRESENTS
THE LETTER
Q

Forgetful Jones

Home:	The Ranch
Favorite Food:	Pineapple upside-down cake
Best Friend:	Clementine
Favorite Pet:	Buster the Horse
Favorite Hat:	Ten-gallon cowboy hat
Favorite Flower:	Forget-me-not
Favorite Song:	"Try to Remember"
Favorite Activity:	Learning poems by heart
Pet Peeve:	Forgetting what he wants to say
Favorite Wish:	To remember what he wants to say
Favorite Saying:	"Uh…I forget."

Who ever heard of a purple pig?
by Grover

*Start at the **purple** man.*

Today I met a **purple** man
Who wore a **purple** wig.
He smiled and said, "I'm **Purple** Dan.
I saw a **purple** pig."

"You saw a . . . **purple** . . . pig?!?" I said.
"Where is the piggy now?"
"Beats me." Dan shook his **purple** head.
"Go ask the **purple** cow."

*Go to the **purple** cow.*

"Oh, **purple** cow, do you know where
The **purple** piggy went?"
"I think," said Cow, "it's over there,
Inside the **purple** tent."

*Go to the **purple** tent.*

I found the tent and went inside
And saw a **purple** duck.
"Where does the **purple** piggy hide?"
She said, "Quack . . . **purple** truck."

*Go to the **purple** truck.*

Now flying 'round the **purple** truck
I saw a **purple** bee.
He buzzed, "Hello, my name izzz Chuck.
You're s'pozzzzed to follow me."

*Follow the **purple** bee.*

I followed Chuck past **purple** trees,
And past a **purple** chair.
I cried, "Where is the piggy, *please?*"
"I know!" said **Purple** Bear.

*Go to the **purple** bear.*

"The **purple** pig lives in a house
That's by a **purple** brook."
So, creeping quiet as a mouse,
I went to have a look.

*Go to the **purple** house.*

I snuck up to the **purple** door
All made of **purple** straw.
I gave 1 knock . . . 2 . . . 3 . . . then 4—
Now guess what Grover saw!

What's inside the house?

Larry DiFiori

GENTE EN MI FAMILIA
PEOPLE IN MY FAMILY

padre
father

madre
mother

abuelo
grandfather

abuela
grandmother

hermana
sister

hermano
brother

hermanita
baby sister

Herry Monster loves to play the piano. He practices every day. He can play almost any type of song. He can play loud and he can play soft. Herry also loves to sing, but he can only sing in one way—very, very loud! Maybe that's why he doesn't have an audience!

Playground Fun

playground

ball

slide

friend

jump rope

swing

seesaw

balloon

How many things in this picture can you "sign"?

Come

play

with   me

OSCAR CHOOSES A PET

"I've been thinking," Oscar muttered,
"Of the pleasant life I lead,
Living in this filthy trashcan—
It is very nice indeed!

But it might be even better
If I had a little pet,
Though it's kind of hard to figure
Just what animal to get."

"I could never think of puppies,
'Cause they wag their tails all day,
And they're lovable and darling,
So I'd hate them right away.

Tiny kittens are no better,
For they're cute, beyond a doubt,
And they're always washing whiskers,
So the kittens, man, are out."

Oscar thought another minute,
Then he almost flipped his wig.
"Holy smoke!" he cried, "I've got it!
I will buy myself a *pig!*

Since a pig is fat and filthy,
I would love him like a cousin.
What a roommate for my trashcan!
Hey! I think I'll buy a *dozen!*"

Grover and Betty Lou, Plumbers

10

Grover Buys Ten Balloons

Qq

The Queer Question Quiz

Hi, everybody.

Guy Smiley here to bring you the moment you've all been waiting for—the Queer Question Quiz! Ladies and gentlemen, I hope you noticed that the words "Queer Question Quiz" all begin with the letter Q. Now, before I ask you today's Queer Question, I want to give you a clue to the answer. Today's answer has a whole lot of Q words in it. And now, here it is, folks—the moment you've all been waiting for—today's Queer Question on the Queer Question Quiz. Today's Queer Question is:

WHAT DID FARMER QUINCY SAY TO HIS PET DUCK QUEENIE WHEN HE WANTED HER TO STOP MAKING NOISE?

Take your time,
think it over. . . .
Okay, folks, your time is up!
The answer to today's
Queer Question Quiz is:

Farmer Quincy said
to his pet duck . . .

QUIT QUACKING QUICK, QUEENIE, AND KEEP QUIET!

Look at all those Q words in one sentence, folks! If that's not enough for you, try saying it five times fast. In the meantime, this is Guy Smiley saying "so long for now" from the Queer Question Quiz! See you again soon. And now, on with the book. . . .

J. Mathieu

Cookie Monster's Number Cookies

GREETINGS! I am **the Count.**

Hello, again. Me **Cookie Monster.** My friend THE COUNT ask me to make special cookies for him. They called NUMBER COOKIES. Ready?

1. Have a grownup heat oven to 400 degrees.
2. Put cloth on table—sprinkle with flour.
3. Roll out dough, about ¼ inch thick, on cloth. (Use dough recipe in volume 1).
4. Cut dough into strips.

5. Use strips of dough to make NUMBERS from one to ten.
6. Put numbers on ungreased cookie sheet and put in oven. Have a grownup help you.

Oh! I can hardly wait!

Well, you gonna have to wait six to eight minutes.

WONDERFUL! I will count the minutes! One minute . . . Ha, ha, ha. Two minutes. Three minutes and counting . . . Four minutes. Five minutes.

Six minutes . . .

Not yet!

Seven minutes. Eight minutes!

O.K.! Now they lightly browned. You want me to wrap them or you going to eat them here?

EAT them? I am not going to EAT them. They are so beautiful, I am going to FRAME them! Wonderful! Wonderful! You are a GENIUS!

Oh, dear. What a *waste.*

Planting a Garden with Ernie

The Count's Birthday Party

Greetings! It is I, the Count. Bert and Ernie have brought me a birthday present. It is a lovely 1 and a beautiful 2.

Here are my presents from Sherlock, Grover and Betty Lou. Just what I always wanted! A 3, a 4, and a 5.

Look! Look! Presents from Roosevelt and his mother, and from Herbert! 6, 7 and 8!

And from Cookie Monster! And from Granny Fanny! 9 and 10! It's wonderful! WONDERFUL!

Now it is time for the party. But first, let us count the guests...1,2,3, 4,5,6,7,8,9,10. Now let us count the presents...1,2,3, 4,5,6,7,8,9,10. Now let us count the candles... Isn't this fun? 1,2,3,4,5,6,7,8,9,10...

pP

The Story of Pete the Pirate

Once upon a time, a nasty pirate sailed into a town. "Ahoy, mateys," the pirate announced. "My name is Pete the Pirate, and I am so nasty that I am going to take away everything in your town that begins with the letter **P**."

And immediately, he grabbed a bag of **peanuts** from the hand of a little girl and dropped it into his pirate sack.

"Heh, heh," chuckled Pete the Pirate, and before he had finished chuckling, he had grabbed a **pizza pie** from the hands of a pizza-maker and had thrown it into his pirate sack.

"There's only one thing you can do to stop me from taking all the **P** things in your town," said Pete the Pirate. "And that's to say a special word that begins with the letter **P**. If anyone says the special **P** word, then I'll stop and go away."

And with that, he picked up a little boy's **puppy** and threw it into his pirate sack.

The people of the town got together and tried to think of what the special **P** word might be. The mayor had an idea. So he marched right up to Pete the Pirate and announced, "**Pickle**!"

"**Pickle**?" said Pete the Pirate. "You think that's the word that will make me stop? Ha!"

And he grabbed the mayor's **pants** right off him and threw them into his pirate sack.

Then, just for good measure, he grabbed the **packages** from the arms of a passing lady, and a stray **pig** that was walking down the street. He threw them in his pirate sack, too.

The people of the town got together again to try to think of the special **P** word that would make the pirate stop taking things. The cook from the biggest restaurant in town had an idea. So when the pirate came into his kitchen, the cook yelled, "**Porcupine**!"

"**Porcupine**?" said the pirate. "You think that's the special word that will make me stop? You're a pretty silly cook, you know that?"

And with that, the pirate grabbed all the cook's **pots** and **pans** and threw them into his pirate sack. Then, just for good measure, he went through the town collecting all the **pillows** and **pianos** and threw them into his pirate sack, too.

Well, the people of the town were getting pretty upset when a little boy came up to the pirate just as he was pulling a **pair** of **pajamas** off the washline.

"Mr. Pirate," said the little boy, "won't you stop taking all the **P** things from our town?"

"Why should I?" said the pirate. "I'm nasty."

"Please," said the littie boy.

"What did you say?" said the pirate.

"I said *please*," said the little boy.

"That's it!" exclaimed the pirate. "That's the special word. **Please** is the special **P** word! I don't like you at all, little boy, but I'll have to stop because you said **please**."

And as quickly as Pete the Pirate had come to town, he left—and he never came back again.

The townspeople were grateful to the little boy. They only wished they had thought of the special **P** word sooner. Still, with the pirate gone, things could return to normal, and the people of the town all lived pretty happily ever after.

PUSSY-CAT AND QUEEN

"Pussy-cat, pussy-cat,
  Where have you been?"
"I've been to London
  To look at the Queen."
"Pussy-cat, pussy-cat,
  What did you there?"
"I frightened a little mouse
  Under the chair."